The YOUNG DASTAN Chronicles

The SEARCH for CYRA

By Catherine Hapka
Based on characters created for the motion picture
Prince of Persia: The Sands of Time
Based on the Screenplay written by Boaz Yakin and Doug Miro & Carlo Bernard
Screen Story by Jordan Mechner
Based on the videogame series "Prince Of Persia" created by Jordan Mechner
Executive Producers Mike Ste
Jordan Mechner, Patrick
Produced by J
Directed by

D1112970

DISNEP PRESS
New York

Copyright © 2010 Disney Enterprises, Inc.
JERRY BRUCKHEIMER FILMS™ and JERRY BRUCKHEIMER FILMS Tree Logo™ are all trademarks. All rights reserved. Unauthorized use is prohibited.

Printed in the United States of America

First Edition
1 3 5 7 9 10 8 6 4 2
J689-1817-1-10182
Library of Congress Catalog Card Number on file.
ISBN 978-1-4231-1784-1
Visit www.disneybooks.com

LONG AGO, in the ancient and sand swept land of Persia, there was a prince whose strength, bravery, and honesty were revered across the land. His name struck fear in his enemies and courage in his men.

This was Dastan.

But before he was to become this prince of legend, Dastan had to survive on the streets of Nasaf, heart of the Persian Empire. It was a place of royal palaces, bustling markets, exotic spices, and beautiful people. But beneath its sleek surface was a rotten underbelly where street kids fought for meager scraps of food and few rules applied.

It is on these streets that the tale of Prince Dastan truly begins. . . .

CHAPTER ONE

Dastan leaned on the sill of the palace window and enjoyed the cool evening breeze. Nasaf lay before him, its rooftops bathed in the coppery glow of the sun setting behind the city's high western wall.

"More dates, Dastan?"

He glanced over his shoulder. His friend Cyra had just hurried in, carrying two platters piled high with food. She set them on the table, which was already groaning under the weight of delicacies of every description—fragrant pomegranates, juicy and succulent kebabs, bowls of steaming rice sprinkled with fresh herbs. The food was piled so high that Dastan could hardly see the luxurious woven rugs hanging on the far wall of the well-appointed sitting room.

"Thanks," Dastan said, stifling a burp. "Where's Ghalander?"

Cyra rolled her eyes as she set down the platters and pushed a strand of dark hair out of her face. "You know him," she said. "He's curious about everything! Now he's asking the palace astronomers whether they can predict the coming of the next solar eclipse."

Dastan chuckled. That indeed sounded like Ghalander. In fact, the other boy's curiosity had led to their friendship—and Dastan's escape from Babylon!*

His smile faded. Why did the thought of the distant city trigger such a feeling of dread

---

*This escape occurred in Volume 1, *Walls of Babylon*.

in the pit of his stomach? Before he could figure it out, a servant entered the room.

"Begging your pardon, sir," the servant said, bowing to Dastan. "Prince Tus and Prince Garsiv are taking an evening stroll through the gardens and would be honored if you would join them."

"Thank you. Since I'm finished, I'll go out and find them now." Dastan glanced at Cyra. "Want to come?"

"I'll join you in a few minutes," she said. "I'm still hungry."

Dastan nodded. Grabbing a handful of dates—after all, he never knew when he'd be hungry again—he popped them into his pocket and headed out. He passed through the palace's maze of rooms and staircases as quickly and easily as he'd once navigated the dusty roof-tops of Nasaf, and he soon emerged into the palace's expansive walled gardens.

Ahhh . . . He couldn't resist stopping to take in the strong scents of the exotic flowering plants King Sharaman had brought in from all over the Persian Empire and beyond. The air was rich with the chirping of insects and the musical calls of unseen birds.

It was all so beautiful it almost seemed unreal. A feeling of peace washed over Dastan as he realized he now had everything he'd ever wished for or dreamed of back when he'd had to struggle merely to survive on the streets. . . .

Then came a soft footstep behind him. Dastan turned, expecting to see the princes, or perhaps Ghalander or Cyra.

Instead, he was just in time to notice the sharp edge of a curved sword swinging toward him! Honed by years on the street, his reflexes kicked in, and he ducked just in time. The metal blade swished right over his head!

"Kazem!" Dastan blurted out as he saw who

wielded the sword—a man who was dressed in the rich robes of Persia's upper classes and had a malicious sneer on his lips.*

"Stand still, boy," Kazem growled. "Can't you see I'm trying to kill you?"

Dastan felt fear and anger rush through him. The man seemed determined to see him dead at any cost!

"You thought you could escape your fate so easily?" Kazem snapped. "You fool."

A chuckle came out of the darkness, and Dastan turned just in time to dodge a dagger as it flew at him. Kazem's cohort Babak stepped into view a second later.

"Young Dastan *is* a silly thing, isn't he?" Babak chortled, clutching his rotund belly with glee. "Still, what do you expect from a lowly Nasaf street rat? He can't even die properly!"

---

* Kazem was the mysterious man who sent Dastan on a dangerous fool's errand to Babylon in Volume 1.

Dastan glanced over his shoulder and saw a third man—Babak's partner, Murdad—swing a rough wooden club toward his head. Beneath heavy brows, Murdad's eyes glittered with malice. Dastan was surrounded! "No!" he cried, somersaulting out of the way.

CRASH! The club smashed down on a decorative birdbath, narrowly missing Dastan and sending shards of stone flying.

Dastan's head was spinning. What were Babak and Murdad doing here in Nasaf? The last time he'd seen them they were in Babylon … halfway across the empire!

Murdad cursed and swung again. Dastan jumped back, tripping over a chunk of the broken birdbath and stumbling into someone behind him.

"Got him!" a familiar voice cried as strong hands grabbed Dastan's arms.

Dastan struggled to break free. By twisting

his narrow shoulders and aiming a sharp elbow into his captor's gut, he managed to wriggle loose and do a quick handspring out of reach.

"Hey!" the same voice cried.

"Titus?" Dastan blurted out, daring a look back.

A pair of youths were staring at him. The taller of the two, Titus, was rubbing his stomach where Dastan had elbowed him. His shorter, hairier friend, Darius, was grinning and looking as stupid and evil as ever.

Titus and Darius were the biggest bullies in Nasaf. But what were they doing in the palace garden?

Come to think of it, what was *he* doing there? That uneasy feeling of dread returned as Dastan realized the men were right. He shouldn't be anywhere near the palace. . . .

"Step aside, all of you," a commanding voice rang out.

"Vindarna!" Dastan stared at the Magian striding toward him, bloodred robes billowing around his tall, thin figure and swirling around his feet.

Vindarna was one of Nasaf's most powerful men, and one of its most mysterious. Dastan's eyes widened as he recognized the two sneering faces behind the Magian. The White Hun princes! They had killed Dastan's best friend, Javed, and nearly finished off Dastan as well.

But what were they doing with Vindarna? They were enemies, or so Dastan had thought, anyway. He'd already known that Babak, Murdad, and Kazem wanted him dead. After finding Vindarna's name among their papers in Babylon, Dastan *had* wondered if the Magian might be in on the plot as well. It appeared he had his answer.*

---

* These events all happened in *The Chronicle of Young Dastan* and Volume 1.

I knew it! Dastan thought, ducking quickly as Babak took advantage of the distraction to toss another dagger at his head. I knew I shouldn't trust him—or anyone!

"Dastan!" a distant voice called out.

He shot a look around at the opponents advancing on him. Kazem was clutching his curved sword. Babak drew out a new dagger. Murdad hoisted his club. Titus and Darius cracked their knuckles and grinned stupidly. Vindarna glided forward, his black eyes boring into Dastan's. And the White Huns muttered to each other in their guttural language as they raised their swords.

"Dastan!" the faint call came again.

This time he looked up and saw Cyra and Ghalander waving at him from a palace balcony. Seeing them together sent another pang of confusion through him. How had the only two friends he had left in the world ended up here in Nasaf together? They didn't even know each other. Besides, Ghalander was supposed to be in Babylon and Cyra at her home even farther away in Bishapur. . . .

"Dastan!" Ghalander called again in his cheerful voice. "Up here, my friend! Dastan! Dastan . . . !"

"Dastan!"

Dastan's eyes fluttered open as Ghalander's call faded away. Someone was shaking him by the shoulder. Opening his eyes, he found himself staring into the bearded face of a young man.

"Are you all right?" the man asked with concern. "You were shouting and moaning as you slept."

"Sorry." Dastan sat up quickly. "Must've had a nightmare."

Reality flooded back as the dream ended.

He was not in Nasaf. He was with a caravan of strangers. Gone were Cyra and Ghalander. Gone were the luxuries of palace life as his fantasies had painted them. And gone, thankfully, were Dastan's enemies. At least most of them, he hoped.

The sun's first thin rays were making their way across the desert sand. All around the oasis, people stretched and yawned as they prepared to start another day's long, hot, dusty journey. The heavy, strong scents of camels and coffee drifted in the morning breeze.

The man who had woken Dastan was Tir, one of his fellow travelers. "Are you sure you're all right?" he asked. "Some of the things you said . . ."

"I'm fine." Spying a beautiful young woman heading their way, Dastan nodded toward her. "I think Laleh is looking for you."

When Tir turned to greet his wife, Dastan

made his escape. He hurried to the edge of the spring and doused his head with cool, clear water, trying to wash away the anxious, helpless feelings his dream had left behind. He couldn't allow himself to become distracted. Vindarna, Kazem, Titus and Darius, the White Huns . . . all were far away in Nasaf, halfway across the sprawling Persian Empire, where they couldn't hurt him or anyone he cared about.

Babak and Murdad were another story. They were still too close for comfort, especially considering that they wanted him out of the picture permanently. Dastan had lost a parchment with his friend Cyra's address on it soon after arriving in Babylon. Later, he and Ghalander had found it in the men's rented room and stolen it back, but that hadn't made him feel much better. Why had Babek and Murdad kept something like that? If they remembered the address, would they come looking for Dastan there now that he'd escaped their grasp?

He couldn't stand the thought of anything happening to Cyra or her family because of him. The girl was impulsive and opinionated and could be aggravating, but she was also smart and loyal—and one of the few people Dastan had ever met who'd treated him as her equal despite his status as a lowly street rat. Even if his worries were for nothing, and Babak and Murdad never showed up, Dastan could think of worse places to hide out for a while than a peaceful horse farm far from everyone who seemed to want him dead. That was why he'd joined this caravan heading toward Bishapur, the city closest to Cyra's family's farm.

He wasn't sure what he'd do if and when he faced any of his enemies again, whether in Nasaf or Babylon or anywhere else. But he wouldn't worry about it too much. If living as an orphan on the pitiless streets of the royal city had taught him anything, it was to think on his feet.

CHAPTER TWO

Hours later, Dastan trudged across the sand beside Tir and Laleh. His natural inclination had always been to keep to himself. But the friendly young couple often invited him to walk with them and sometimes even share their food—a welcome bit of generosity for Dastan. Thanks to Babak and Murdad, he'd lost most of the money Kazem had paid him before he set out for Babylon. Now he traveled with only the clothes on his back and a few leftover coins, most of which had already gone to pay the caravan leader.*

＊ Ironically, the fee that Dastan was paid by Kazem in the *Walls of Babylon* was payment to send Dastan to his own death.

Today, he was not good company. He was having trouble focusing on his companions' conversation. His nightmare lingered in his mind, distracting him from everything else. Dastan didn't normally believe in omens or prophecies. He found plenty to occupy him in the real world of hunger and hardship without resorting to fantasies of magic and mystery. But for some reason, he couldn't quite shake the idea that his dream had meant something. . . .

"I'm weary of traveling," Laleh said with a sigh, squinting against the merciless midday sun. "I can't wait until we reach Bishapur."

"Me, too," Dastan mumbled, trying to shake off his thoughts. "It's been too long already, and I need to get there before . . ." Suddenly realizing he might have said too much, he let his voice trail off. "I'm weary of traveling, too," he finished with a shrug.

Laleh nodded understandingly. Then she

glanced at her husband. "Tir, I'm feeling faint with thirst. Could you fetch me a cupful of water from the pack camels?"

"Of course." Tir hurried off.

When he was gone, Laleh smiled at Dastan. "Perhaps you can take my mind off my thirst and boredom by telling me more about yourself?"

Dastan smiled back shyly, rather dazzled by her beauty. Women like Laleh never paid him any notice back in Nasaf. They looked right through him if they happened to pass him on the street, as if he were no more important than a stray dog or a pigeon. "There's nothing interesting to tell," he said uncertainly.

"Oh, come now." Her smile broadened, and she tilted her head to one side and gazed at him. "Surely a boy with eyes as intelligent as yours has many tales to tell!"

Dastan felt his cheeks go red. "No, really," he protested weakly. "My life is very dull."

"Your waking life, perhaps." Laleh chuckled. "But I hear your dreaming life is quite active. Full of swordplay and mysterious enemies in Babylon . . ."

Dastan gulped, feeling foolish. "Did Tir tell you that?"

She nodded. "He said it sounded as if you were making some daring escape, perhaps even from Babylon itself?" She smiled at him indulgently, as if he were a child. "As if you could do such a thing!"

"But I did! Really!" Dastan protested before he could stop himself.

"Really?" Laleh laughed and clapped her hands. "I knew it! I told Tir you had the look of a hero, but he insisted you were just an ordinary boy."

Dastan bit his lip. This was a sticky situation. He knew that he still had a chance to cover his tracks if he wanted to. He could tell her Tir was right, that it had happened only in his dreams. That he was just an ordinary street rat from Nasaf who'd never done anything special. But looking into her almond-shaped brown eyes, seeing that dazzling smile aimed at him, he just couldn't resist. He had fantasies of one day meeting a woman as beautiful as Laleh and sharing his adventures with her. It was a far-fetched fantasy, though. So why not at least take this one chance . . . ?

"Tir is wrong," he bragged. "I *did* escape from Babylon, even with the entire city guard trying to stop me."

Her mouth formed a little O of surprise. "You did?" she exclaimed. "Oh, I can't wait to tell Tir! He'll be so impressed!"

As quickly as it had come, Dastan's moment of bravado faded, replaced by the uncomfortable feeling that he'd said too much. But what was the harm? Laleh still didn't know the whole story. And she'd given him no reason to distrust her. . . .

"Please. Just don't tell anyone else what I've said," he said. "I—um, I don't like attention."

"Of course." Laleh smiled. "Your secret is safe with me."

The sun was dipping toward the horizon when the caravan reached their next destination and could finally stop for the night. The sprawling but sparse oasis was located in a rough, rocky part of the desert, with only a few spindly palms and some scratchy-looking brush surrounding a shallow, meandering spring-fed stream. A small settlement had sprung up around the spring at one end of the stream. It consisted of a trading post, a rustic caravansary with a large pen for the camels, and about half a dozen dusty, low-slung houses. The whole place had a sleepy air. The only signs of life were an old man squatting beside a fire and drinking coffee; a skinny, sand-colored dog who let out a few lazy barks when it spotted the camels; and numerous flies buzzing around the entrance to the trading post.

Dastan had avoided Laleh and Tir for the rest of that day's journey, still feeling a lingering sense of uncertainty about opening up. This, he thought, was why it was better to keep to oneself. You never had to worry about what you said or didn't say, how it could be used against you. Seeing the couple head straight for the trading post, he made himself useful tending to the camels until Laleh and Tir wandered off again.

Then he headed over to the trading post himself. It was little more than a few dusty tables shaded by a large tent. His stomach grumbled as he ducked inside. Waving away the flies, he surveyed the food available for purchase. He pulled out the pouch where he kept his dwindling supply of money. When he put his hand in it, he gulped. There was only one coin left.

"Can you make change for this?" he asked the trader, showing him the coin. "I'd like to buy that bread."

"Certainly." The trader was a shifty-eyed fellow with a sparse black beard. "Wait here while I fetch your change."

He ducked out the back of the tent. Dastan set his coin on the table, then picked up the bread and took a bite. It was dry and a bit stale, but after the day's journey it tasted delicious.

As he lifted the bread to his mouth for another bite, the trader burst back in. Two large, burly men were with him.

"That's the boy," the trader said, pointing to Dastan.

"Hey!" Dastan cried as the other men grabbed him. The bread flew out of his hands and bounced onto the sand. "What are you doing? Let me go!"

CHAPTER THREE

"Let me go!" Dastan cried again as the men dragged him out of the tent.

"Quiet, boy," the trader said. "It'll go easier for you if you don't fight."

"But I paid for the bread!" Dastan protested. "Why are you doing this?" His mind raced with terrible possibilities. Was this trader working for Kazem? Spotting Tir and Laleh standing nearby, he shouted, "Help me!"

Tir and Laleh glanced at him, their expressions blank. "This the boy you meant?" the trader called to them.

"Yes." Laleh glanced briefly at Dastan before returning her gaze to the trader. "That's the one."

The trader nodded, then pulled out a few coins and gave them to Tir. "Pleasure doing business with you," the trader said.

Dastan stared at Tir and Laleh, still not understanding. Neither of them would look at him. Tir tucked the money away, then led his wife off without a backward glance.

The trader strode over. "Lock him up and keep an eye on him," he ordered his men. "We'll need to keep him safe until I can get a message to Babylon. If those two weren't telling tales, someone there should be very interested in our new prisoner."

Dastan's eyes widened as he realized the truth. Tir and Laleh might not know the specifics about what had happened to him back in Babylon, but thanks to his noisy dreams and his big mouth, they *did* know he'd escaped from the Babylonian guard. And it seemed that was enough. They must have figured out that there could be a price on his head and had sold that information to the trader.

He'd been tricked—again! "Let me go!" Dastan howled in rage.

He kicked at the thugs holding him, connecting with one man's knee. "Ow!" the man yelped, grabbing a dagger from his belt. "You'll pay for that one, you urchin!"

The trader grabbed the knife wielder's arm. "No!" he said, his eyes flashing angrily. "We need him alive!"

Dastan took advantage of the momentary distraction and pulled away. "Hey!" the other goon holding him exclaimed.

But Dastan, slick as a fish slipping through the waters of the Euphrates, had already wriggled out of his grasp. He dashed off, ducking back into the tent.

"Get him!" the trader cried.

Dastan sprinted through the tent, scooping up another piece of bread on his way. After all, he'd paid for it, and then some. . . .

He burst outside and found himself staring down the main street of the village—if the rutted, sandy path between houses could be called a street. It was dinnertime, and the scent of food filled the air. A few women were bent over cooking fires in front of the houses, and a scruffy goat nibbled at a patch of brownish grass sprouting in the middle of the street.

"Stop that boy!" one of the burly men shouted, barreling out of the tent behind him.

Dastan raced down the street, dodging the fires. People started to emerge from their houses, drawn by the shouts and commotion.

But Dastan didn't stop, hurdling the surprised goat and skidding around the next corner. The stream lay before him, broad and shallow as it tumbled away from the village. On the far side of it was the caravansary. The leader of Dastan's caravan was helping the locals herd the camels toward the pen where they would spend the night. It was nothing more than a hard-baked patch of desert, shaded by a few palms and enclosed by a rough clay wall. Several curious horses were peering over the wall, watching as the stubborn camels tried to stop and graze on the sparse greenery outside the enclosure.

Dastan heard more shouts coming fast behind him. Back in Nasaf, he could outrun nearly any pursuer by taking to the rooftops, which he knew better than most people knew the city's streets.

But here? A quick glance at the roofs told him it would be pointless. They were as flat and featureless as the desert itself, and too few in number to get him very far.

Just then, one of the camels let out an irritated bleat as a worker pushed it toward the pen. That gave Dastan an idea.

"Aaaaah!" he yelled, splashing through the stream and racing wildly toward the small herd of camels milling around outside the gate.

"Stop! What are you doing?" the head of the caravan cried.

Dastan ignored him, his eyes seeking out the smallest and fastest-looking camel of the bunch. When he was a few yards away, he gathered momentum by flinging himself forward into a series of handsprings. Then he launched himself upward—onto the camel!

The animal snorted in alarm, taking a quick step backward. Unfortunately, Dastan came up short of the spot he was aiming for on the beast's back and barely managed to wrap his arms around its hairy neck on his way down. A split-second later the camel spun around and took off.

"Hey! Get back here!" someone yelled.

Dastan couldn't look back to see who. It was all he could do to hang on as the camel lumbered away from the village, swerving around the few palm trees and assorted rocks as it gathered speed.

"Whoa!" Dastan gasped as his body flopped helplessly against the camel's side. His eyes widened when he saw that they were approaching a fairly deep, wide section of the stream, which had twisted back toward them, creating a loop of water around the village before it meandered its way into the desert. "Slow down!" he cried.

SPLASH! The camel galloped into the stream. That seemed to finally bring it back to its senses. It stopped suddenly, bent its head to take a drink, and in the process flung Dastan into the cold water.

"Thanks a lot," he muttered, sitting up and wiping his face.

Hearing shouts, he glanced over his shoulder. The trader and his goons were running toward him, along with the caravan leader and five or six villagers.

Dastan jumped to his feet in the middle of the stream. The camel's wild bolt had given him a head start—but not much of one.

Grabbing the camel's still-lowered neck, Dastan launched himself onto the creature's back once again. This time he actually landed in the right spot. He gave the camel a kick with both heels.

"Come on, I thought camels never needed to drink," he shouted. "Giddyap already!"

The camel lifted its head, and turning its long neck, shot him an annoyed look. But at

Dastan's continued urging, it finally ambled out of the stream and started walking at a slightly faster pace.

Dastan was relieved—until he glanced back and saw the trader and some of the others grabbing several of the penned horses!

"Faster!" he shouted, kicking his camel again. "Please!"

The camel ignored him, continuing at the same moderate gait. Dastan glanced back again, just in time to see the trader and several other men swing up onto horses and ride after him. At this rate, they would catch up to him in no time!

The situation was growing dire. The stream was still visible to Dastan's left, but it was much narrower here, and after a few dozen yards it disappeared into a rocky area of large boulders and the occasional scrub tree. Dastan leaned that way, hoping the camel would pick up the hint and turn. It did, though slowly, pricking its ears toward the sparse bits of greenery growing among the rocks.

Dastan thought the rocky area might offer a hiding place. But his heart sank when he saw that it was only about fifty yards wide. After that, all he could see was plain, flat desert stretching away toward the setting sun on the horizon.

Still, he couldn't give up. If the villagers returned him to Babylon ...

He wished he hadn't lost so much of Kazem's reward. If he still had even half of it, maybe he could have bribed the trader into letting him go. But there was no point in wishing. He would have to rely on his wits, and luck, now. Reaching into his robe, he pulled out the hunk of bread he'd grabbed on his way through the tent. It was a little soggy after his dunking, but still in one piece.

Dastan jumped off the camel as it rounded the largest of the boulders, which hid them from view of the village. As soon as his weight left its back, the creature shuffled to a stop. "Good boy," Dastan whispered.

Working fast, he broke a couple of long twigs off one of the scrubby trees. As the camel grazed, he wedged the sticks into the sides of its halter so they stuck straight out in front of its nose. Then he slipped out of the robe he'd been wearing, pausing for a second to run his hand over the fine fabric.* He hated the thought of leaving it behind.

But he hated the thought of being captured even more, so he tossed the robe onto the camel's back and shaped it into a vaguely rider-shaped lump, hoping the clinginess of the wet fabric would keep it in place long

---

* Ghalander gave Dastan the robe to wear in order to disguise him as a Babylonian in Volume 1.

enough to fool his pursuers.

Dressed only in the tattered rags he wore beneath the robe, Dastan reached up and stuck the chunk of bread onto the ends of the sticks protruding in front of the camel's nose.

The smell of the soggy bread woke up the creature immediately. Its eyes opened wider as it snuffled at the treat now dangling several inches beyond the end of its nose. The camel's long tongue emerged, reaching for the treat and coming up just short.

"Go get it!" Dastan urged, first tipping the camel's head in the direction he wanted it to go, then giving the animal a sharp slap on the rump.

The camel burst into motion, stretching its neck forward eagerly. It headed straight out into the desert, running faster and faster as it tried to catch up to the bread. Dastan watched it go, feeling both amused and a little bit guilty about the trick.

Then he heard the sound of hoofbeats. He dove behind a boulder a split second before the trader galloped into view.

"There he is!" the man shouted as he spotted the camel, which was at least a hundred yards away now and moving faster than ever. Though it was starting to slip to one side, the lumpy robe was still in place.

Dastan held his breath as half a dozen horses thundered past his hiding place. He could only hope the fading light and the camel's hunger would keep the game going a little longer. In the meantime, he needed to figure out what to do next—and fast.

He crawled out from behind the boulder and looked around, hoping he'd missed something the first time. But all he saw were a few boulders and smaller rocks tumbled across the sand like a child's forgotten toys.

Wait—what was that? He squinted toward

a dark area at the base of the largest boulder. It was a cave!

The squeal of a horse startled him out of his thoughts. He jumped, realizing the posse must be returning already. Without thinking, he dove into the cave.

As soon as he did, he realized he might have made a fatal error. The villagers had to know about this place. It wouldn't take long for them to figure out where he was. And while they most likely knew how to navigate the cave, it was foreign to Dastan.

Peering out, he saw most of the horsemen already trotting into view. They stopped at the edge of the rocky area and sat there atop their horses, talking quietly among themselves.

A minute or two later the caravan leader appeared, leading the camel behind his horse. He stopped beside the others and glanced around.

"He must be hiding in there," he said loudly, nodding in the direction of the cave.

One of the villagers hushed him, shooting a nervous look around. Then he leaned closer, murmuring something that Dastan couldn't hear. Another man stared directly at the cave entrance, his expression troubled.

Dastan backed away quickly to avoid being spotted. He glanced around, wondering if there might be another way out of this cave. The place was pitch black, offering no clues to its size or shape. Could he possibly find some hiding spot that the men might miss? Then again, maybe it would be better to dash out and try to get behind them without being spotted. . . .

To his surprise, when he looked out again, he was just in time to see the last of the men riding back toward the village.

He felt the faintest stirring of hope. He

shook his head. "Yet, why would they leave when they know I'm in here?"

Then a voice spoke out of the darkness, and Dastan's hopes vanished. "Those villagers be fools," it said. "But not foolish nor bold enough to venture into a known den of thieves."

CHAPTER
FOUR

Dastan spun around, his heart racing, just as a light flared behind him. Standing in the back of the cave were half a dozen raggedly dressed but well-armed men flanked by several large dogs.

Outlaws! Dastan gulped as they circled him, coming closer and closer. One of the dogs let out a low growl.

"Easy, Onager," the man who'd spoken before said with a chuckle. He was tall and lean, with cunning black eyes and an ugly scar on one cheek. "Don't eat him until we find out if he's got anything of value."

"Right." A burly fellow with a bristly beard nodded as he fingered his dagger lovingly. "I'd hate to have to cut open one of our own dogs to retrieve only a few coins."

That made all the men laugh loudly. A couple of the dogs howled along.

"I—I have nothing of value," Dastan said in a voice that was shakier than he would have liked. "You might as well let me go."

"Nothing of value, hmm?" The scarred man smirked. "Then how do you expect to buy your freedom?" He glanced at his comrades. "What are we to do with him? There's no meat on him. It's hardly worth the effort to cut him up and feed him to the dogs."

A third man, shorter and stouter than the rest, stepped forward. When the light hit his face, Dastan saw that he had only one eye. Where the other had been there was now only an ugly patch of wrinkled skin.

"We might be able to use him as a decoy once we reach Sardis," the one-eyed man said.

He reached out and poked Dastan with the tip of his sword. Dastan reacted on instinct, jumping straight up and somersaulting over the sword. Landing beside the bristly bearded man, he plucked the dagger out of his hand before he could react. Then Dastan spun around and faced the thieves, dagger at the ready.

"Hey!" the bearded guy complained.

But the scarred man laughed, grabbing his dog just as it tried to lunge at Dastan. "Well done, my small friend!" he exclaimed, his eyes twinkling. "It seems you're not like those soft, fearful villagers after all."

"Indeed," the one-eyed man said, looking impressed as well. "We should have guessed by the rags he wears that he's not one of them. He seems more like one of us!"

"I'm Surin, the leader of this ragtag crew," the scarred man said.

"*You're* the leader? Says who?" grumbled the bearded man. "Zirak should be the leader— he's the smartest."

"Give it a rest, Kav," Surin ordered. Then he smiled at Dastan. "Sorry about that, lad. We were only joking when we said we'd feed you to the dogs."

"Yes," the one-eyed man said drily. "Surin is a great lover of jokes."

"Well, we can't all be serious thinkers like you, Zirak." Surin winked at Dastan as Zirak rolled his one good eye. "He's just holding a grudge because I tricked him into sitting on an anthill last week."

Zirak's hand strayed to his backside, and he began scratching. "'Tis true, I didn't find that very amusing," he said sourly.

But Surin and the rest of the men laughed

uproariously. Kav, clearly enjoying his friend's discomfort, gave Dastan a slap on the back so hearty that he nearly stumbled forward.

"What'd you do to get those villagers after you?" Kav asked.

Dastan's mind raced. The last time he had told the truth it came back to punish him. He wouldn't, no, he *couldn't* make the same mistake again.

"I, uh, stole that camel," he said. "You see, I needed to get to Bishapur as quickly as possible, and the caravan was moving too slowly."

"Stole a camel in broad daylight, eh?" Zirak said. "Not sure if that makes you brave or stupid, but either way you'll fit right in here."

Surin chuckled. "Indeed. We're heading to Susa in the morning if you'd like to ride along that far. From there, it's only a short trek on to Bishapur."

"I could steal you a horse," Kav volunteered eagerly, rubbing his meaty hands together. "That camel of yours ain't being brought to your door anytime soon."

One of the younger thieves laughed. "There's nothing Kav loves more than stealing horses."

Dastan hesitated for only a moment. These men were pretty rough around the edges, but they seemed like a good-natured lot. If they could get him away from the village and closer to Cyra's farm at the same time, why not take the chance and join them?

"Thanks," he said. "By the way, my name's Dastan."

Early the next morning while Surin and the others were boiling coffee over a campfire, Kav slipped away in the direction of the village.

"Don't worry, Dastan," Surin said. "He'll choose you a fine mount. Kav may not be anyone's idea of a genius, but he has an eye for horseflesh."

"I'll fetch the other horses, Surin," one of the younger thieves offered.

He hurried out of the cave and off in the opposite direction, along with two other young men and a couple of the dogs. Dastan gulped down his coffee, then set about helping dismantle the camp.

Before long the young men returned, leading six fine-looking horses. "Come. Help saddle up, Dastan," Zirak said as he hoisted a saddle onto a bay stallion.

Dastan hesitated. "Er, I will if you'll show me how to do it." He shrugged. "I have little experience with horses, I'm afraid."

Surin heard him and raised an eyebrow. "I see. Well you'll learn soon enough if you wish to keep up with us. We don't have time for stragglers."

"I'll keep up," Dastan assured him. "I've ridden before a time or two. Just never done the saddling."*

Zirak was showing him how to attach the saddlebags when Kav returned from the village riding a flashy black mare. "These desert folk may be timid fools, but they have some nice horses," he said as he brought the mare skidding to a halt. "I had trouble choosing!" As he dismounted, the horse tossed her head and began to rear. Kav laughed and gave her a pat.

"Nice work, Kav. I like a horse with spirit." Surin glanced at Dastan. "Ready to give her a try, boy?"

Dastan gulped, staring at the mare as she pawed the sand. She looked a lot more fiery than he'd expected. But he wasn't about to let the men see that he was nervous.

＊ The first—and only—time Dastan found himself on horseback was in *The Chronicle of Young Dastan* when running from the White Huns.

"I'm ready," he said with as much bravado as he could manage.

But he'd barely climbed into the saddle before he found himself on the ground again, not sure what had just happened. All the men were laughing loudly as they watched the mare, who'd bucked him off with ease, trot a few steps away.

"Bravo!" Kav cheered, clapping his hands. "That was a lively show to wake us up this morning, Dastan."

Dastan groaned and climbed to his feet. "Glad you appreciated it," he said drily, which made the men laugh again.

Determined not to give up, he brushed himself off and headed toward the mare, who'd joined the other horses. But Surin held up a hand to stop him.

"I like the looks of that mare," he said. "Sorry, Dastan, but I insist upon trading mounts."

"But . . ." Dastan began, not wanting to look weak.

"I warn you, don't argue with me, boy." Surin raised an eyebrow. "You take my horse—the gray stallion over there."

Dastan shrugged, feigning annoyance. But beneath it he was relieved—and grateful to Surin.

Sweat beaded on Dastan's face and dripped down his back. He'd been riding with the thieves for hours in a haze of hot, sandy sameness, and some of his gratitude had faded. Luckily, the black mare had given Surin little trouble, and the gray stallion had given Dastan even less—he was a well-trained, agreeable creature who seemed willing to go wherever he was pointed.

Dastan was relieved to have left the oasis village behind. He should have known better than to trust anyone on that caravan! When he thought of the way Laleh had smiled and cajoled him into telling her his secrets, he wanted to pound his head against a wall for being such a fool.

"Doing all right, Dastan?" Surin called as he steered his flashy mare past Dastan's horse. The dog, Onager, loped along at the mare's heels.

"Fine, thank you," Dastan replied. "When will we reach Susa?"

"Very soon, my boy," Surin replied.

Kav heard them and nodded. "And from there, on to Sardis!" he exclaimed. Most of the others let out a ragged cheer.

"What's in Sardis?" Dastan asked, realizing they'd mentioned the city a couple of times. He had only a hazy idea of geography but was almost certain that Sardis was many, many days' journey from this part of the empire.

For a second nobody answered. Finally

Zirak broke the silence. "Merely another heist," he said. "That's all."

Dastan shrugged. Sardis seemed like a long way to travel for an ordinary heist. But he wasn't concerned with the thieves' plans. He'd just spotted the outline of a large city on the horizon.

Surin saw it, too. "What'd I tell you? Looks like we're coming to Susa. We'll buy provisions, then take the main road northwest toward Sardis."

"And I shall leave you there," Dastan spoke up. "I am heading in the other direction, to Bishapur."

The thieves all traded looks. Surin cleared his throat. "Are you sure, Dastan?" he said. "This Sardis heist is going to be tricky, and you've already proved yourself quick-witted and bold. We could use someone like you."

"You want me to come with you?"

Dastan was surprised. He wasn't used to feeling wanted or appreciated—at least not since Javed had died. In a strange way, he felt flattered.

"Think about it, Dastan," Kav urged. "This Sardis heist is going to be a big one. You would have riches beyond your wildest imagining!"

Dastan opened his mouth to say no but hesitated. The offer *was* tempting. But was this really how he wanted to attain such riches? By turning himself into a professional thief? Besides, Cyra was in danger because of him. He couldn't forget that.

"It sounds like a fine adventure, and I thank you for the offer," he told the thieves. "But I have important business near Bishapur."

For a second Surin looked annoyed. Then he shrugged. "It's your choice, Dastan," he said. "Farewell, and perhaps one day we'll see you again."

Dastan nodded, though he already wondered if he was making the right decision. But they'd reached a signpost marking a crossroads. There was no time left.

"Good luck in Sardis," he said.

Then, turning his horse, he headed down the road toward Bishapur, while the thieves headed into Susa without a backward glance.

Both Dastan and the horse were hot, thirsty, hungry, and exhausted by the time they reached Cyra's family farm. They'd left the arid desert a couple of days before and entered an area of rich farmland, rolling foothills, and thick forests.

Upon reaching the more populated area near Bishapur, Dastan pulled out the directions Cyra had given him. The skills he had learned on the streets didn't include reading, but by asking other travelers for help he'd found his way to this lush but isolated valley.

Now he paused to look down over it,

enjoying the peaceful scene of well-kept horses grazing in the fields that circled the tidy farm buildings. The idyllic surroundings made Dastan feel grubby and a little uncertain. True, Cyra had invited him to visit anytime. But what would she say when she saw him? Or heard why he was there?

"Doesn't look like Babak and Murdad beat me here, at least," he murmured to himself, seeing no signs of anything amiss. "Perhaps they aren't coming after all."

The horse stamped his foot and nosed at a patch of grass. Dastan gave him a pat and let up on the reins so the horse could snatch a bite to eat.

"I'm hungry, too," he said. "Let's find somewhere to wash the desert sand off both of us and get some real food." He had decided to offer the fine gray stallion to Cyra's family. He only hoped that the gift would serve as sufficient apology for putting them in danger.

It didn't take long to find a cold, clean stream tumbling down from the peaks of the Zagros Mountains. Dastan offered the horse a drink and then washed up, enjoying the feeling of being clean.

Leaving the stallion tied to a branch so he could graze along the stream bank, Dastan returned to his lookout spot.

But when he gazed down at the farm, the scene had changed. It was no longer tranquil. A woman and a young boy were carrying buckets of water to the horses. And watching them, a sword in his hand and a wary look on his round face, was ... Babak!

Dastan gasped. He was too late!

He watched the woman stop and pat one of the horses. That had to be Cyra's mother— she had the same lush dark hair and spirited expression as his friend.

Babak was watching her, looking impatient. He said something—Dastan was far too distant to hear what—and waved his sword threateningly. Tipping her chin up, Cyra's mother swept past without a word and went into the house with the little boy scurrying behind her.

Dastan crept along the back wall of the farmhouse, holding his breath. Reaching a window, he peeked inside. The room was empty, so he ducked his head and moved on.

It was just after sunset. Dastan had left the gray stallion tied in the hills, then sneaked down to the farm on foot. There were a couple of men posted at the side of the house near the drive, but they had been leaning on the fence watching the horses. Dastan had had no trouble slipping past them without being noticed.

He paused at the next window. If he could only find Cyra . . .

Dastan put his head down almost as soon as he'd raised it. This room was occupied—but not by Cyra. Babak and Murdad were both there, along with several other scary-looking men. They sat around a broad wooden table and appeared to be involved in a raucous game of knucklebones.*

"Loser of this round has to clean up after the horses!" one of the men roared gleefully.

"Agreed," Babak's voice rose above the guffaws. "And to make it interesting . . . winner gets the honor of roughing up the street rat when he shows up."

"*If* he shows up," Murdad growled. "I still have my doubts. Why would this place mean anything to him? A street rat like that has

---

* Fun trivia! Knucklebones is an ancient game similar to jacks or dice; it is played with pieces of bone usually taken from sheep.

no honor and no real friends."

Dastan scowled, tightening his fists. Who was Murdad to throw stones? What did he know about him or his honor? Nothing but whatever nonsense Kazem had told him. What's more, all Kazem knew of Dastan seemed to come from some silly prophecy Ghalander had found mentioned in the men's papers—and only a fool would give credence to something like that.*

He moved on, more carefully than ever. The next room was empty, but soft voices drifted out of the one after that. Dastan peered in; the woman he'd seen earlier was braiding a girl's hair while two small boys played in the corner. Another girl, a year or two younger than Cyra, folded clothes nearby, but there was no sign of Cyra herself.

---

* This happened in Volume 1, *Walls of Babylon*—though Dastan and
Ghalander weren't able to figure out much about this mysterious
prophecy before they had to run for their lives.

Dastan took a deep breath, glancing back toward the other window. He could still hear the men talking and laughing over their game. He hoisted himself up and went through the window, hoping that nobody inside would scream or call out in surprise when they saw him. He landed, finger to his lips in a gesture of silence.

It worked. None of them made a sound, though they all looked startled and wary. Dastan stepped toward the woman, holding his hands out so she could see he had no weapon.

"My name's Dastan," he whispered. "I'm a friend of Cyra's. Is she here?"

"Dastan? The boy from Nasaf?" The woman's eyes widened. "My daughter said you might come! She's told us all about your adventure together."

"Yeah," one of the boys said. "We didn't believe most of it."

"Hush, child," his mother chided gently. Then she turned her dark, worried eyes back to Dastan. "You should go. If those men see you here . . ."

"I know." Dastan shot another look around the room. "But where's Cyra? Did they hurt her?"

Cyra's mother shook her head. "They arrived yesterday evening," she whispered. "They took us captive—all but Cyra, who managed to slip away without being seen."

The older girl nodded, clutching a robe to her chest. "Cyra is very brave," she whispered. "She sneaked out of here on horseback and is riding to warn Father."

"Yes," her mother said. "My husband and our older sons were away delivering some horses when the marauders came."

Dastan sagged with relief. Cyra was safe. Still, he had brought all this trouble upon her family. He feared there might not be time to fix everything. . . .

At that moment a door behind him burst open. "What's all the noise in here?" Murdad demanded.

CHAPTER
SIX

Dastan froze. His back was to the man, and his eyes darted to the nearest window. Should he leap toward it? He was fast, and he had the element of surprise—he was pretty sure he could get away. But what would that mean for the others?

"Well?" Murdad said. "Answer me!"

Wait! He hadn't recognized him yet! With his back to him, how could he? Dastan was small and slight enough to pass as one of the younger children. At least until Murdad took a better look . . .

"Oh, you startled us!" the older sister exclaimed with a laugh. Smooth as the wind, she stepped past Dastan toward Murdad. On her way, she casually dropped the robe she was holding over Dastan.

He clutched the soft fabric around himself, keeping his head down and not daring to move. Meanwhile, the girl was practically skipping toward the door.

"You see, we were deep in a discussion about what to serve you for tonight's meal," she told Murdad earnestly. "Mother thinks we ought to have rice with broad beans, but my brothers don't like broad beans much. They say they taste like dirt. We keep telling them they're not in charge of the menu, but, well, you know how little boys are . . ." She laughed merrily. "At least I suppose you must! You were once one yourself, weren't you? Did you enjoy broad beans at that age?"

"What are you on about?" Murdad growled irritably. "Hush your incessant chatter, child! I'm not interested in a discussion of beans. Just keep it down from now on, will you? All of you."

There was the sound of stomping feet, fading away quickly. A few seconds later Cyra's mother let out a breath. "Quick thinking, Asha," she told her daughter. "Dastan, I think he's gone."

Dastan shot Asha a grateful smile as he handed back the robe. "Thank you," he said. "If he had recognized me . . ."

"Don't think about that," Cyra's mother said. "You need to go before he comes back."

Dastan nodded. "I will. But only so I can ride out and help Cyra and the men. Together, I'm sure we can come up with a plan to defeat the marauders."

"Yes," Cyra's mother agreed. "Perhaps you can alert the neighboring farms as well. They're too far away to have realized anything's wrong, but they're good people. I know they'll help."

Dastan nodded, feeling more hopeful. After some quick directions from Cyra's mother and a last whispered good-bye, he vaulted out through the window.

Minutes later, he was climbing the steep hill by the light of the rising moon. But when he reached the stream bank where he'd left his horse, he got a nasty shock.

The stallion was gone!

Dastan spun in a circle, wondering if he was going insane. Where could the horse be?

A closer look at the branch where he'd tied the creature gave him an answer of sorts. It was snapped off halfway to the trunk!

"Must've spooked and pulled himself loose," Dastan murmured. "But where'd he go?"

The obvious answer popped into his head

immediately. Horses were herd animals—he'd seen the way they pressed together with their own kind when they were frightened. Hurrying to the overlook, he peered down.

Sure enough, the stallion was grazing among the other horses, his gray coat gleaming in the milky moonlight. Dastan gulped as he noticed the broken branch still dragging from the stallion's halter. The marauders might not notice an extra horse, but if any of them caught sight of that . . .

Besides, Dastan needed his horse back if he was to have any hope of finding Cyra and the others before they returned. He skidded back down the trail into the valley and vaulted over the pasture fence.

"Here, boy," he called softly as he hurried toward his horse. The field held about a dozen others, all of them relaxed and grazing in the cool night air.

The gray stallion lifted his head, watching Dastan approach. When he was a few paces away, the horse turned and trotted slowly in the opposite direction, the broken branch swinging against his neck with each step.

Dastan let out a groan and followed, hoping the men were too busy to glance out the window. The stallion turned behind another horse and stopped, dropping his head to graze again.

"Good boy," Dastan muttered, creeping around the second horse, who eyed him warily. "Just let me grab your . . ."

The stallion flung up his head, thwarting the boy's attempt to grab his halter. The broken branch swung wildly and smacked into the other horse, making it snort and bolt in fright. That roused the rest of the herd.

In moments, all the horses had stopped grazing and had either raised their heads in alarm or started racing around. The noise, to Dastan, was deafening.

He shot a nervous look at the house. His heart was pounding nearly as loudly as the horses' stomping hooves. Would the men hear the commotion and come out to investigate? Should he wait and see or act? He was wasting valuable time.

Still, he forced himself to be patient and wait for the herd to settle. Once they did, he tried once more to catch his horse. This time he got close enough to grab one end of the branch stuck in the beast's halter. The stallion tossed his head, nearly gouging out his own eye. Then, the branch came loose. With a soft groan, Dastan tossed it aside.

"I give up," he told the hind end of the rapidly departing gray stallion. Then he looked around at the other horses. Selecting a pleasant-looking bay mare, he stepped toward her cautiously.

She lifted her head from the grass but made no move to escape as Dastan took hold of her halter.

He let out a sigh of relief. But it caught in his throat as he heard a door creak open. Ducking behind the stout body of his mare, he peered at the house. One of the thugs was standing there, staring out at the pasture. Could he see Dastan from that angle?

"Looks all right out here, boss," the man called after a moment. "Just the horses running around, I guess."

He went back inside and closed the door. Dastan vaulted aboard the mare, not wanting to waste any time. He would ride her up the hill bareback to fetch the tack he'd taken off the stallion earlier.

"Come on, girl," he whispered, guiding her toward the nearest gate with gentle pressure from his heels. "Let's get out of here."

CHAPTER SEVEN

By the time the sun rose the next morning, Dastan had been riding for several hours. The mare he'd chosen had a smooth gait and an agreeable disposition, and that allowed Dastan plenty of time to think. But he was beginning to wish he didn't have quite *so* much time. His thoughts were dark. All he could see were Cyra's mother and siblings being held prisoner by the ruthless Babak and Murdad.

The landscape he rode through was rough and varied. Thick, forested areas were interspersed with farmland, and all of it sloped upward toward the distant mountains. It was very different from the desert landscape Dastan was used to, but the scenery was lost on him because of his quest. He'd decided to stick to the main road, since Cyra's mother thought that was the way Cyra and the others were most likely to return.

Around midmorning, Dastan stopped to let his horse drink from a shallow stream that tumbled along the right side of the road. As he dismounted and shook the stiffness out of his legs, he heard a humming noise from around the next bend in the road. He glanced toward the sound, uneasy at the way the trees hid that part of the road from his view. At least in the desert you could see what was coming....

He led his mount into the shelter of thick trees to the left, just in case. Then he eased farther down the road, keeping to the edge of the forest. Even as he did, he felt foolish. This was a well-traveled road—he'd passed any number of riders and pedestrians already. But he still felt the need to be careful. What if more thugs were coming to join Babak and Murdad at the farm?

When he rounded the last few trees he saw a girl standing there, humming while she watched a sturdy chestnut horse drink from the stream. Her back was to him, but Dastan would have recognized her anywhere.

"Cyra!" he called out in relief.

She spun around, arm raised. Dastan ducked when he saw that in her hand she held a dagger in throwing position.

"Whoa! Hold on! It's just me!" he exclaimed. "Don't throw that!"

Cyra's jaw dropped along with the hand holding the dagger. "Dastan?" she asked.

He grinned. Cyra wasn't an easy girl to

surprise, and he was somewhat proud of himself for doing so.

"Good thing it's only me," he said. "If I'd been an enemy, you never would have heard me coming. I'm amazed you managed to survive on the streets of Nasaf as long as you did."

She rolled her eyes. "Very funny. What are you doing here? Did you walk all the way from Nasaf?"

"That's kind of a long story. But no, I didn't walk. My horse is this way." Dastan led Cyra around the curve in the road. The bay mare had wandered out of the woods to nibble at some grass along the edge of the stream.

"Is my family all right? Did you talk to them?" Cyra demanded with sudden urgency.

"They're fine," Dastan said. "But how did you know I came from your farm?"

Cyra let out a laugh. "Do you think I don't recognize one of our own horses?" she said, hurrying over to pat Dastan's mare. "But enough chitchat. My father and brothers should be heading this way—we'll be able to intercept them within the day."

Dastan nodded, smiling despite the desperate situation. He'd nearly forgotten how bossy Cyra could be—and how tough, clever, and capable, too. Everything else aside, it was nice to see her again.

"And you still don't know why this Kazem character is trying to kill you?" Cyra asked.

Dastan shook his head. The two of them had been riding along the road for about an hour. It had taken him that long to tell her everything that had happened since he'd seen her last—meeting Kazem in Nasaf, the trip to Babylon, Babak and Murdad, the horse thieves, and the rest.

"I have no idea," he said with a sigh. "The

only clue we have is what Ghalander and I found in Babak and Murdad's papers. Some nonsense about a prophecy."

"What kind of prophecy?" Intrigued, Cyra turned in the saddle to stare at him.

Dastan sighed again. She'd always been more willing to believe in superstition than he was. Then again, she'd grown up on that beautiful, peaceful farm. She hadn't had the hard streets of Nasaf to teach her to trust only what she could touch, taste, or see.

"I don't really remember," he said. "Just the usual claptrap about ancient relics and journeys to faraway lands and such. Nothing to do with me."

"Clearly those men think it's got something to do with you. Otherwise, why would they be trying so hard to kill you?"

Dastan didn't answer. He'd just noticed a cloud of dust in the distance. "Looks like a big group coming fast," he said. "We'd better move aside or risk getting run over."

They steered their horses to one side of the road. As the cloud of dust drew closer, Dastan could see only the vague shapes of several horsemen. Then the lead rider skidded to a halt in front of them.

"Stand and deliver!" he shouted. "If you have any coins about you, we'll thank you to hand them over!"

Cyra groaned. "Highwaymen!" she spat out, her eyes flashing. "Just what we need."

But as the dust settled, Dastan peered at the riders. "Surin?" he blurted out. "Kav? Is that you?"

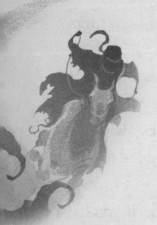

CHAPTER
EIGHT

"Dastan!" Surin roared happily. "Look, men! It's our young friend!"

Dastan's head spun. He'd never expected to see those outlaws again. They should be well on their way to Sardis by now! he thought. Surin's dog, Onager, leaped forward to eagerly sniff Dastan's foot, making his mare prance nervously.

"What are you doing here?" Dastan blurted out. While he no longer feared the thieves, he *was* slightly nervous about them being there with a purpose he might not like. What if they'd decided they couldn't spare his help after all and were going to forcibly "convince" him to join them?

Dastan shook off the thought as quickly as it had come. They'd been kind to him thus far. And if they planned to seize him, they were showing no signs of it yet. Instead, Surin was peering at his mount, looking anxious.

"What happened to the gray stallion?" he asked, his voice sounding strained. "I hope you weren't robbed by some unsavory horse thieves and lost beast and tack alike!"

Dastan didn't bother to point out that Surin and his men were horse thieves themselves. "Nothing of the sort," he replied. "Your horse is safe and sound at Cyra's farm if you want him back."

"Don't be a fool, boy," Kav growled. "It's not the horse we need—it's our maps!"

"Maps?" Dastan shook his head, confused. "What maps?"

Meanwhile, Cyra was staring from Dastan to the thieves and back again, looking confused. "Hold on," she interrupted loudly. "What's going on here? Dastan, are these the men you told me about? They're so ... dirty."

Surin raised an eyebrow as he looked her over. "Who's the feisty young lady, Dastan? She looks a bit too finely bred to be spending time with someone like you."

"She's a friend," Dastan said. "And we're actually in a bit of a hurry. If you'll just explain about these maps of yours, I can help and ..."

"Surin was impulsive and thoughtless, as usual," Zirak interrupted. "He traded horses with you, never bothering to recall that our maps of Sardis were in your saddlebags. We were a day's journey along before we realized it."

Kav nodded. "Without those maps, the

heist is impossible. That's why we came back looking for you."

"Oh!" Dastan laughed, relieved. "Don't worry. I may have lost the horse, but not the saddle—or the saddlebags." He gestured at his tack, which he'd removed from the gray stallion before it escaped.

Surin swung down from his horse and hurried over. He dug into Dastan's saddlebags and soon found the maps. "We're back in business, men!" he roared happily.

"It's about time." Zirak rolled his good eye. "Now let's get back on the road to Sardis."

"Wait," Dastan blurted out as an idea occurred to him. "Since you're here, we could use your help. You see, some men are holding Cyra's mother and younger brothers and sister hostage. We're riding to find her father and older brothers, but we'll need to defeat them when we get back...."

Surin looked sympathetic as Dastan outlined the rest of the situation. But then he shook his head.

"Sorry, Dastan," he said. "Coming for these maps has already put us several days behind schedule. But is this why you were in such a hurry to reach Bishapur? To save some family's farm?"

Zirak nodded, glancing at Cyra. "Your young lady friend is pretty, but not pretty enough to throw away our offer."

"He's right," Kav put in. "Come with us, Dastan! You won't regret it when you have more money than the king himself."

Cyra scowled at them. "Dastan doesn't need your thieving ways," she told them hotly. "He's better than that!"

Any slight temptation Dastan might have felt disappeared at her words. Could she truly see such good in him? Javed had always claimed so, but Javed was gone now and . . .

"Sorry, guys," he told the thieves, deciding to believe in himself, at least this once. "I appreciate your offer. But this is something I need to do."

Surin shrugged. "Your choice. Perhaps our paths will cross again someday, young Dastan." He put a hand on Dastan's shoulder and peered deep into his eyes as though searching for an answer to a question Dastan didn't know he had been asked. Then, he squeezed his arm and leaped back on his horse before adding over his shoulder, "In fact, I think it is destiny that we shall meet again. So for now, no good-byes." Turning, he signaled to his men. "Come on, fools. We have what we came for."

Dastan watched as they turned and galloped off, the dogs howling at their heels and Surin's words ringing in his ears. All this talk of destiny lately. What could it mean? And was Surin right? Would they meet again? Was *that* his destiny? To one day be a part of their group.

Shaking his head clear, he sighed. That would never happen. He wouldn't let it. Cyra had said he was better than that—and he hoped to prove her right.

Dastan watched as Cyra's father, a tall, lean, weather-beaten man named Abadan, peered out over the farm from an overlook in the hills.

"I don't see anything happening down there," Abadan reported. "Everyone must be inside."

Cyra's oldest brother, Adel, clutched his sword. "Good," he said. "That gives us the element of surprise. So let's go get them."

"I'm with you," his brother Adro put in, and the third brother, Advi, nodded eagerly. All three young men were tall, broad-shouldered, and brave. Dastan had found them a little intimidating when he and Cyra had finally met them on the road. They reminded him of the bold young men who always looked upon him with disdain—if they noticed him at all—back in Nasaf.

But on the journey back to the farm the boys had quickly made him feel like a long-lost brother, and Dastan realized that the entire family considered him a hero for looking after Cyra when she'd run away to Nasaf. That was a weird feeling. Despite all his dreams of a grand future, Dastan had never thought of himself as any kind of hero.

"Wait," Cyra told her brothers. "Dastan and I already told you, there are tons of men down there. If we just go marching in, there will be a bloodbath."

"We?" Advi eyed her with a smirk. "Who said you could come along, baby girl?"

"Baby?" Cyra echoed with a scowl. "I'm only

a year younger than you, Advi, and ten times as smart!" Then she spun to face her father. "We need a plan," she said. "Perhaps one of us should ride for reinforcements while the others get closer and scout out the situation at the farm."

Abadan nodded thoughtfully. "I think you're right," he said, raising a hand to silence his sons as they started to protest. "But let's wait to send word to our neighbors until we know exactly how much of a threat our enemy is."

"I'll sneak down and scout it out, Father," Adel volunteered eagerly.

"No," Dastan blurted out before Abadan could respond. "Let me do it. I sneaked down once before."

"No, me," Adro said. "No offense, Dastan, but this calls for someone older and stronger."

"Don't be so sure, my cocky brother," Cyra put in with a frown. "Dastan has survived by

his wits on the streets of Nasaf for a long time.
I wonder if any of you could do the same."

Advi snorted with laughter. "I could, but not
Adro," he said. "He'd be whining for his own
soft bed within an hour."

"Silence." Abadan's tone was mild, but the
boys quieted immediately. "Dastan, are you
certain you want to do this?"

Dastan nodded. "It's the least I can do for
bringing this trouble upon your family."

He stood up straight, forcing himself to
meet Abadan's eye steadily as the man looked
him up and down. Finally Abadan nodded.

"I think you are the right one for the task,
if you truly wish to accept it," he said. "But be
careful."

"Good luck, Dastan," Cyra whispered.

Dastan shot her a small, tight smile. Then
he nodded to the others and slipped off down
the hill.

A few minutes later he was creeping along the side of the house once again. It felt much riskier in broad daylight—if one of the guards posted at the entry road wandered around the corner, he'd spot him immediately.

But Dastan tried not to think about that. He'd just heard a burst of loud laughter coming from one of the windows. The closer he got, the more raucous the commotion. Sliding along the wall, he carefully stood up and peeked in.

Babak and Murdad were inside, along with at least half a dozen of their thuggish guards. A long table was loaded with all manner of food—grilled kebabs, soups and stews, fresh naan, countless rice dishes garnished with fruits and vegetables. There also appeared to be plenty of wine, which the men were enjoying a great deal.

Watching the party, Dastan felt a flash of hope. It looked as if most, if not all, of the thugs were here in one room, distracted by their fine meal. If he could let the others know, perhaps there was a chance they could trap them. . . .

He spun around but stopped short when he found himself face-to-face with a dagger. It was being held by a well-dressed man with a tidy beard.

Kazem had found him!

CHAPTER NINE

Kazem smirked at Dastan's startled expression. "Very gracious of you to greet me upon my arrival from Nasaf," he said. "I wouldn't have expected such manners."

Frozen with surprise, Dastan stared at Kazem—the man who had set up a complex and far-reaching plot, seemingly for the sole purpose of having him banished or killed. Dastan wanted to ask him why, but his tongue seemed just as frozen as the rest of him.

"Speechless with joy at seeing me, eh?"

Kazem's smirk broadened. "I heard you escaped your fate in Babylon, so I came right away. Looks as if those two buffoons can't even handle a simple task like doing away with you. I'll have to take care of it myself."

That broke Dastan out of his stupor at last. He twisted quickly aside, avoiding Kazem's grasp. Then he dodged around him and vaulted over a stone wall.

WHOOOOSH!

Dastan ducked behind the wall just in time. Kazem's dagger flew past over his head— then seemed to stop in midair before plunging straight down at him!

Dastan flung himself to one side.

THUNK!

The dagger became embedded in the ground, missing Dastan's right leg by inches. Dastan gulped. Kazem was no ordinary merchant or nobleman. Back in Nasaf, Dastan had seen him cut off someone's ear with a move so quick Dastan's eyes hadn't been able to follow it. It might have seemed like magic—if Dastan believed in such things.*

Whether real or magical, Dastan didn't like being the focus of Kazem's dagger-throwing skills. He burst out of his hiding place like a flushed hare and sprinted across the nearest field.

"You can't escape your fate, boy!" Kazem howled.

Dastan ran even faster, zigzagging among the grazing horses, all the time expecting Kazem's dagger to catch him in the back. As he plunged into the trees at the base of the hill, his relief at escaping turned to despair. There was no way they'd be able to surprise the marauders now. . . .

"Never mind," Abadan said when he heard

* This occurred in Volume 1, *Walls of Babylon*.

what had happened. "The battle was coming one way or another. Now we must prepare to fight."

Stepping to the overlook, Dastan glanced down. Already men were pouring out of their houses, clutching their weapons and shouting.

Dastan nodded. He was ready.

A short while later, Dastan and Cyra were crawling through the tall grass of an unused field. "We need to get to the stable," Cyra hissed in his ear. "There are some spare weapons stored there."

Nearby, a shout went up. Lifting his head slightly, Dastan was just in time to see Adro dash out from behind a tree and bring the handle of his sword down on a thug's head. The man crumpled to the ground, and Dastan smiled grimly. Kazem's men might be large and well-armed, but they seemed poorly prepared for this battle, having partaken in a little too much food and drink.

His eyes widened when he saw another goon hurtling toward Adro, sword raised. Dastan let out a yell, and Adro spun around. At the same time, Dastan grabbed a stone and hurled it at the thug. It connected with the villain's arm just as he started to bring his sword down toward Adro's head. The man howled with pain and the blow went wide, allowing Adro time to disappear back into the trees.

The thug glanced after him, then yanked his bow from his belt. He notched an arrow, turning to squint toward Dastan and Cyra.

"Run!" Cyra cried.

They raced off toward the nearest patch of trees, ducking the arrows that soon came flying their way. Dastan felt one graze his arm, but he didn't slow down until he and Cyra were both in the shelter of the trees.

* * *

The battle raged on for some time after that. Cyra's father and brothers stayed hidden in the trees and outbuildings, dashing out just long enough to attack one guard or another. Dastan watched it all from his hiding spot in the main stable building, which he and Cyra had reached unseen by crawling across a field behind a low stone wall. He was itching to go out and help, but he'd promised Cyra's father that he'd stay with her.

Soon, one brother after another came dashing into the stable to join them. Advi had a bloody nose from a brief struggle with one of the thugs, and Murdad had nicked Adel's arm with a dagger. But the boys were otherwise unhurt.

Finally Abadan joined them, tumbling into the barn through a window. "Everyone all right?" he whispered.

"We're fine, Father," Cyra replied. "But we need a better plan. We'll never defeat them at this rate!"

Before Abadan could respond, they heard a shout from the direction of the yard behind the house.

"What's that?" Advi whispered.

Dastan crawled over to a crack in the wall and peered out. His eyes widened when he saw what was happening. Kazem had just dragged Cyra's mother out of the house and was holding a sword to her throat!

"Come out, wherever you are!" Kazem called loudly. "If you don't show your faces, you can say good-bye to this good woman!"

"Mother!" Adro whispered in horror, pressing his face to the wall so he could see as well. "We have to save her!"

"Wait," Abadan hissed. "That man has no honor. If we go out, he might simply kill us all—and your mother along with us."

Dastan knew Abadan was right. Once again, he was reminded that this was all his fault. If he hadn't lost Cyra's address, these terrible men would never have come here. He felt sick.

"Stay here," he said, realizing what he had to do. "I'll give myself up. Maybe that will satisfy them."

Abadan shot him an appreciative look. "I'll go, too," he said. "They don't know how many more of us there are. If Dastan and I can convince them there's only the two of us left . . ."

"But they'll kill you, Father!" Cyra exclaimed, clinging to his arm.

Adel nodded. "There must be another way. . . ."

As the others continued to argue, Dastan peered out again. Cyra's mother was standing erect, her face expressionless and her eyes dry. Then he spotted the younger children huddled in a doorway nearby. The little ones were sobbing, and tears poured down Asha's face even as she tried to comfort them.

Dastan shifted his gaze back to Kazem's impatient face. There was no more time to waste.

"Here I am!" he shouted, pushing past Abadan and through the stable door. He hurried into the open. "Please don't hurt her."

Kazem spun to face him, and an evil smile spread across his face. "Hello again, Dastan," he said. "I'm glad to see you."

With a gulp, Dastan realized that Kazem didn't care about Cyra's family at all. *He* was the only one Kazem wanted.

Dastan took a step toward Kazem and then another, his heart pounding but his resolve firm. Kazem watched him approach, looking pleased.

Suddenly there was a clatter of hoofbeats

coming around the corner of the house. "Hey," a new voice called out. "What's going on here?"

Dastan spun around, along with everyone else. His jaw dropped.

"Ghalander?" he blurted out in amazement.

CHAPTER
TEN

Indeed, it *was* Dastan's friend Ghalander, the clever, curious student who had helped him escape from Babylon. He was mounted on a fine chestnut mare and flanked by a pair of burly, well-armed guards on large, stout black warhorses.

For a second nobody moved. Cyra's mother was the first to recover from the surprise of the new arrival. She yanked free of Kazem's grip, pushing herself away from him.

"Get back here!" Kazem snarled, going after her with his sword raised.

The blade seemed to glide down toward her in slow motion. Without thinking, Dastan flung himself into its path, shielding Cyra's mother with his own body. He wanted to avoid seeing the killing blow heading toward him, but he forced himself to keep his eyes open. He might be a humble street rat, but he would look death in the face with the dignity of a king. . . .

At the last second, Kazem's face twisted in anger, and he wrenched the sword aside so that it landed harmlessly in the dirt instead of splitting Dastan in two. Dastan gasped with relief and surprise. The man had missed him on purpose. Why? Didn't Kazem want him dead? Wasn't that what this was all about?

There was no time to wonder. Cyra's mother had already leaped to her feet, ducked under the pasture fence, and run behind the body of the nearest horse, a fiery-looking chestnut stallion. As Kazem yanked his sword blade free, Dastan jumped away, too.

Kazem's eyes shot from Dastan to Cyra's mother and back again. Dastan could read the calculation in the man's eyes. He could go after Dastan, who was the one he really wanted but was also the one more likely to outrun him. Or he could try to grab Cyra's mother again and lure Dastan back that way. . . . A second later Kazem turned, vaulted the fence, and ran toward Cyra's mother, dodging in front of the stallion.

But the sudden movement spooked the horse, and it reared and struck out. Its front hooves caught Kazem just behind his shoulder, sending him flying like a child's cloth doll. He crumpled to the ground and lay still. Babak let out a cry of alarm and rushed forward, while Murdad and the other men looked on, stunned.

Dastan spun around. "Ghalander!" he cried. "Help us!"

Ghalander had been watching the scene in confusion. Now his mind cleared, and he turned to speak to his guards. At the same time, Abadan and his sons came pouring out of the stable, weapons at the ready. Cyra was behind them, inserting an arrow in her bow. Dastan saw Kazem's sword lying nearby and grabbed it. It was heavy, but he was pretty sure he'd be able to make good use of it. Out of the corner of his eye, he spied a thug coming at him. He used the sword as a balance so he could do a quick handspring and get out of the way. Then he swung the sword around, aiming for the man's midsection.

"Oops!" he said as the sword missed its mark and flew out of his hand, its weight too much for him to hang on to. The thug laughed, but not for long. Dastan jumped straight up, aiming a kick at his face. With a grunt, the man went down flat on his back.

"Nice one, my friend!" Ghalander's cheerful voice called out.

Glancing over, Dastan saw that Ghalander and his horse had already waded into the fray. The mare had just trampled a goon, who now lay groaning on the ground, while Ghalander was battling another with his sword.

Dastan grinned. "You're doing pretty well yourself, my friend," he called, before turning to face another enemy heading his way.

After that, it was all over pretty quickly. Babak remained distracted by Kazem's prone form long enough for Cyra to knock him over the head with her bow. Murdad put up a better fight, wielding two swords at once, but he was finally overpowered by Adel and one of Ghalander's guards. Even the younger boys helped by shooting stones with their slingshots.

The thugs seemed unwilling to continue for long once their leaders were captured, and they soon surrendered.

Everything was chaotic for a while as Dastan, Ghalander and his guards, and Cyra's family tied up their prisoners. Advi volunteered to ride off and fetch some neighbors who could help them transport the thugs to justice. In all the commotion, it took a few minutes for Dastan to realize that one prisoner was missing.

"Where's Kazem?" he asked Cyra.

She glanced around and shrugged. "I don't know," she said. "Last I noticed, he was still unconscious."

"Me, too. But now I don't see him anywhere."

Dastan spun on his heel, searching the faces of the prisoners. He saw Murdad scowling darkly in the corner and Babak talking fast, clearly trying to convince Adel and Adro to let him go even as they tied him up. But there was no sign of Kazem.

"How could he have escaped?" Dastan murmured.

Cyra shrugged again. "He seems like a spooky guy. And maybe a bit . . . magical. You did say that dagger he threw at you seemed to turn in midair."

"Don't be silly. There's no such thing as magic." Dastan frowned, feeling uneasy. He hurried over to check with Abadan. After calling his sons over, Cyra's father confirmed that Kazem did indeed seem to be absent.

"Never mind," Abadan told Dastan as he tightened the ropes around a goon's arms. "I doubt he'll be back."

Dastan wasn't so sure. There was such evil in his eyes. Such a thirst for violence.

Yet . . . he couldn't help remembering the way Kazem had redirected that killing blow.

Why hadn't he finished him off when he'd had the chance?

"Thanks, Dastan." Abadan smiled and released a horse into the stall Dastan had just cleaned. "You didn't have to clean out the whole stable by yourself. Why didn't you ask Advi to help?"

"I don't mind." Dastan gave the horse a pat. It had been several days since they'd defeated the marauders, and he was already settling into the rhythm of the farm. "I like to work."

Cyra hurried into the stable, followed by Ghalander. "There you are, Dastan," she said. "We've been looking everywhere for you! Mother asked us to go out and gather some mushrooms for dinner."

"Yes," Ghalander said eagerly. "Cyra prom-ised to show me how to tell which are the good ones and which are the poisonous ones."

"Only if you're nice to me," Cyra teased.

Dastan smiled. He was still amazed at the way the two had hit it off. He was also amazed that Ghalander didn't seem to bear him the slightest ill will, even though he'd been kicked out of his school in Babylon under suspicion of helping Dastan escape from the city. Nobody had dared do anything to him beyond that due to his family's wealth and power. But now, suddenly left with nothing to do and with few friends in Babylon, Ghalander had decided to pay a visit to his uncle, who lived near Bishapur. He'd hired the two guards to help him get there through the lawless desert.

"And of course I remembered that address we found," he had told Dastan with a grin. "I suspected you might go there to check on your friend, so I figured I'd stop by and see if you'd made it."

"Good thing you did," Cyra had put in as she

listened. "Otherwise who knows what might have happened."

Dastan thought about that now as he followed his friends out into the fields behind the main pasture. He had to admit he was enjoying his stay with Cyra's family. They were treating him and Ghalander as honored guests, and they seemed willing to overlook the fact that it was Dastan's fault their lives had been disrupted. Adel and Ghalander were even teaching Dastan to read a little better, while Adro was helping him with his swordsmanship. And of course it was nice to have a comfortable bed and plentiful food for a change. Part of Dastan thought he could stay here forever and be perfectly content.

But another part of him couldn't forget that Kazem was still out there somewhere.

He did his best to put the thought out of his mind. A short while later, Cyra came in with a basketful of wild mushrooms, and he realized he was hungry. Then a sharp cry from overhead interrupted the fun. Peering up into the bright midafternoon sky, Dastan saw a bird hurtling toward them.

Dastan jumped back just in time, as a weary-looking falcon crashed down in the exact spot where he'd just been standing. "Oh!" Ghalander exclaimed as the bird flapped its wings weakly. "Poor thing looks like it's had quite a journey."

"Look—it's carrying a message." Cyra pointed to a tiny bit of parchment curled around one of the falcon's legs.

Ghalander gently took the bird in hand, cooing to it soothingly. The falcon was too exhausted to put up a fight as Ghalander detached the tiny bit of parchment and unfolded it.

"Dastan!" he exclaimed as he scanned the parchment. "It's a message—for you!"

"Are you trying to make a joke?" Cyra grabbed the parchment. "How in the world would a bird find him like that?" Then her eyes went wide. "Oh! I see."

"What is it?" Dastan demanded.

Ghalander read aloud over Cyra's shoulder: "It says, 'Dastan—please come immediately—I am held prisoner in the fire temple at Ghagha-Shahr. Only you can save me and the world. Vindarna.'" He glanced up. "Vindarna—isn't that the name we saw in those papers?"

"Vindarna is the one who saved Dastan and me back in Nasaf," Cyra explained. "It sounds like he's in big trouble!"

Dastan felt his idyllic mood shatter. He stared at the note, his head spinning. "Yes, he saved us once," he said. "But Kazem claimed him as a close friend, and as Ghalander says, we saw his name in Babak and Murdad's papers."

"Dastan, he needs you!" Cyra protested.

"You owe Vindarna your life—we both do. We have to help him now in return. There's no other honorable choice."

He nodded slowly. "I suppose you're right," he said. "I'll have to leave for this Ghagha-Shahr—wherever it is—in the morning."

"I'm coming with you," Cyra said immediately.

"Me, too," Ghalander added. "For one thing, I actually know how to get to Ghagha-Shahr. That might help." He laughed.

"No!" Dastan stared at them. "You two have faced enough danger because of me. In case you haven't noticed, I seem to attract trouble wherever I go."

Ghalander shrugged. "What else do I have to do?" he said. "My parents are furious that I've been kicked out of school. I'm in no hurry to return to Ctesiphon."

"Mother and Father won't want me to go," Cyra said. "But I don't care. Vindarna helped me when I needed it. I'll do the same for him."

Dastan opened his mouth to argue. But the stubborn looks on his friends' faces stopped him. Since when had either of them ever listened to his advice, anyway?

"Fine," he said wearily. "*We* leave for Ghagha-Shahr in the morning."

Journey from the desert to the sea and join young Jack
Sparrow's crew on their earliest adventures in . . .

The Quest for the
Sword of Cortés

by Rob Kidd

Based on the earlier life of the character, Jack Sparrow,
created for the theatrical motion picture,
"Pirates of the Caribbean: The Curse of the Black Pearl"
Screen Story by Ted Elliott & Terry Rossio and Stuart Beattie and Jay Wolpert
Screenplay by Ted Elliott & Terry Rossio,
and characters created for the theatrical motion pictures
"Pirates of the Caribbean: Dead Man's Chest" and
"Pirates of the Caribbean: At World's End"
written by Ted Elliott & Terry Rossio

Available wherever books are sold in 2011

CHAPTER ONE

A dim moon rose over the ocean as the wind blew thickening clouds across the sky. Faint shadows were cast up on the island below: huge, black sailing ships, sea monsters, and other things that haunted the midnight waters seemed to cascade over the hills. Few stars were strong enough to twinkle through the stormy haze. The white sands of the beach were swept into little whirlwinds, shifting the patterns on the sand dunes.

A bad night for sailing.

The few respectable citizens of Tortuga stayed snug in their well-guarded houses. Everyone else—buccaneers, swashbucklers, and cutthroats all—was down at the Faithful Bride, drinking ale and rum.

Between gusts of wind from the gathering storm, the noise from the tavern could be heard a half mile away. Laughing, shouting, and the occasional burst of gunfire echoed through the night as drinkers took up a chanty they all knew:

> Yo ho, yo ho, *a pirate's life for me!*
> *We kindle and char and inflame and*
>   *ignite—drink up me hearties, yo ho!*
> *We burn up the city, we're really a*
>   *fright—drink up me hearties, yo ho!*
> Yo ho, yo ho, *a pirate's life for me . . .*

From outside, the Faithful Bride looked

like nothing more than an oversize shack. It wasn't even built out of proper wood, but from the timbers of wrecked boats. It smelled like a boat, too: tar and salt and seaweed and fish. When a light rain finally began to fall, the roof leaked in a dozen places.

Inside, no one seemed to care about the puddles on the floor. Tankards were clashed together for toasts, clapped on the table for refills, and occasionally thrown at someone's head.

It was crowded tonight, every last shoddy chair filled in the candlelit tavern. *I reckon we have enough old salts here to crew every ship in Port Royal*, the Faithful Bride's young barmaid, Arabella, thought. She was clearing empty mugs off a table surrounded by men who were all hooting at a story. Like everyone in the pub, they were dressed in the tattered, mismatched garb common to all the "sailors" of the area: ragged breeches, faded waistcoats, stubbly beards, and the odd sash or belt.

One of them tugged on her skirt, grinning toothlessly.

Arabella rolled her eyes and sighed. "Let me guess," she said, tossing aside her tangled auburn locks. "Ale, ale, ale and . . . oh, probably another ale?"

The sailor howled with laughter. "That's my lass!"

Arabella took a deep breath and moved on to the other tables.

"There's no Spanish treasure left but inland, ye daft sprog," a sailor swore.

"I'm not talkin' about *Spanish* treasure," his friend, the second-rate pirate Handsome Todd said, lowering his voice. There was a gleam in his eye, not yet dulled by drink. "I'm talkin' about Aztec Gold, from a whole *lost kingdom*. . . ."

Arabella paused and listened in, pretending to pick a mug up off the floor.

"Yer not talking about Stone-Eyed Sam and *Isla Esquelética*?" the sailor replied, skepticallly. "*Legend* says Sam 'e had the Sword of Cortés, and 'e cursed the whole island. Aye, I agree with only one part of that story—that it's *legend*. Legend, mate. 'A neat little city of stone and marble—just like them there Romans built,' they say. Bah! Rubbish! Aren't nothing like that in the Caribbean, I can tell you!"

"Forget the blasted kingdom and the sword, it's his *gold* I'm talking about," Handsome Todd spat out. "And *I* can tell you, I *know* it's real. Seen it with my own eyes, I have. It changes hands often, like it's got legs all its own. But there are ways of finding it."

"Ye got a ship, then?" the first sailor said with a leery look in his eyes.

"Aye, a fine little boat, perfect for slipping in and out of port unseen . . ." Handsome Todd began. But then he noticed Arabella, who was pretending to wipe something from the floor with her apron. She looked up and gave him a weak smile.

She looked again at the floor and rubbed fiercely with the edge of her apron. "Blasted men, spillin' their ale," she said.

Handsome Todd relaxed. But he looked around suspiciously as if the other buccaneers, the walls, or the King himself were listening. "Let's go somewhere a bit quieter, then, shall we? As they say, *dead men tell no tales.*"